THE BRIDE OF FRANKENSTEIN

BY

JOHN L. BALDERSTON

British Library Cataloguing-in-Publication Data
A catalogue record for this book is available from
the British Library

Contents

JOHN L. BALDERSTON

John L. Balderston was born in Philadelphia in 1889. He attended Columbia University, and began his career in journalism as the New York correspondent of the *Philadelphia Record*. In 1915, he moved to England, where he worked as editor for *The Outlook*, and during World War I he worked as a war correspondent in Europe. Balderston authored his first play, *The Genius of the Marne*, in 1919, and he followed this with *Morality Play for the Leisured Class* (1920), *Tongo* (1924), and *Berkeley Square* (1926), a ghost story that was very popular in both London and New York.

In 1927, Balderston talked Bram Stoker's widow, Florence, into selling the American dramatic rights to *Dracula* to producer Horace Liveright. In thanks, Liveright hired Balderston to modernize the novel for the stage, and Balderston adopted a somewhat radical approach, even going so far as to add and remove characters. Published by Samuel French, Balderston's version has gone on to become the most influential of the many dramatic versions of *Dracula*, having been staged and adapted numerous times.

Balderston's *Dracula* led him into a screenwriting career, initially for Universal Pictures horror films. In addition to *Dracula*, he contributed to *Frankenstein*, *Bride of Frankenstein*, *The Mummy*, and *Dracula's Daughter*. He was also on the team of writers who worked on the famous 1939 adaptation of *Gone with the Wind*. During this later period of his life, he garnered two Academy Award nominations. Balderston retired to Beverly Hills, California, and died some years later, aged 64.

The Bride
of Frankenstein

By JOHN L. BALDERSTON

PROLOGUE

HAVE YOU FORGOTTEN how the Monster 'died' – or what the Monster was? Perhaps you never even heard the prologue to this hideous tale?

Read then, that you may better understand the most fantastic history in the world – and remember that to-day men are still striving for the same goal that Frankenstein achieved, and with similar, if not yet equal, success.

Frankenstein, the brilliant young scientist, had defied the laws of nature. He had unravelled the very secrets of Heaven. He had made – a man!

Man? – well, perhaps that term was generous. Nevertheless it was by that name that he hailed his creation in the first flush of his success.

For months he had worked in secret. Everything had been thrust aside while he slaved for the fulfilment of his dream – to create a living man from the bodies of the dead. Even Elizabeth Lavenza, his betrothed, had been forced to endure his neglect while her lover remained behind the locked doors of his great laboratory.

Gradually, rumours began to spread through the surrounding villages. There were whispers of ghouls at work in the churchyards. Body snatchers. Vampires.

A frightened peasant ran screaming to the mayor with a fantastic story of a newly opened tomb, and a dead man who sat propped inside a coach while a cloaked figure with glaring eyes urged on his horses as though all the devils in Hell were after him.

Corpse after corpse was stolen from the grave before Frankenstein's horrible experiment was completed. His handsome face grew white and lined under the terrific strain. But at last the moment came when with a trembling hand he pressed the vital lever – and only *he* knew with what feelings he watched the result of his handiwork rise moving from the operating-table.

Afterwards had followed a period of terror. This was no Man – but a Monster! True, it was fashioned in the semblance of a man, but there the likeness ended. Turning on its creator it broke loose, transforming the peaceful countryside into a shambles.

Night after night came tales of a monstrous shape that stalked the lanes; a giant frame reeking of the tomb, whose rags but ill-concealed the grave-worms crawling in their folds. It moved and gibbered – so said report – for it could not speak. Its yellow skin scarcely covered the muscles and arteries beneath, and its dun-hued watery eyes bleared sullen murder.

Sweethearts wives, honest yeomen and innocent children, all had fallen lifeless beneath its steely fingers. Frankenstein's Monster spared none. Grateful indeed was the scientist that nobody outside his one immediate circle knew that he was responsible for the death-dealer's existence.

Then, just before this tale commences, the strangest piece of irony occurred. On Frankenstein's own wedding day the Monster appeared. As he and Elizabeth left the church together, the creature struck him down, and trampling all who got in its way, fled roaring out of the village. Emboldened by their numbers the villagers set out in pursuit, trapping the creature in a deserted windmill. With oil-soaked rags they fired the place.

And as the flames roared upward, they saw the Monster, overcome by the fumes, fall back into the fire.

Thus rises the curtain on this most horrid sequel.

ONE

Night was casting her shadows over the little village of Ingolstadt – *and the Monster was dead!*

Around the smouldering ruins of the old mill the villagers still shrieked their hate, but mingled with their shouts were cries of joy. At last it would be possible to sleep in peace. The terror had been destroyed.

At the side of the little hillock topped by the glowing wreckage, an old man and woman were standing. They had been there all day, waiting for the end. Now, his eyes crazed with pain as those of a maddened bull, the old fellow stared dumbly at the Monster's pyre.

A charred beam fell with a crash on to the smoking heap. The embers stirred and glowed, and a new flame leaped sky-ward. The old man's lips moved, and he shook off the woman's detaining hand fiercely.

His words came in a groan of anguish: 'Maria! My daughter – my little girl! IT killed her!'

Tenderly his wife put her arm about him. Her own grief was forgotten in her fear for his reason.

'Come home, Hans,' she urged him. The Monster is dead now. Nothing could live through that furnace. Why stay here longer?'

He shook his head. A shower of sparks spat venomously up at the night sky from the crackling beam lying athwart the ruin. Once more his lips parted.

'I must see him with my own eyes,' he muttered, as one who spoke to calm his own soul. 'If I can but see his blackened bones – I may sleep at nights.'

Slowly he made his way towards the ruins.

One by one the villagers were departing, urged homeward by the burgomaster. They went in little groups, for few could summon the courage to walk alone at night so soon after the nightmare had passed. Soon only the woman was left to watch the smouldering pile and the stumbling, halting figure of her good man.

With faltering footsteps the old fellow made his way to the edge of the burned-out mill. The villagers had done their work well. The heat was terrific. Hans felt the dense smoke slewing on the breeze, prick at his old eyes till the tears came. For his child he could not weep. Some sorrows cut too deep.

A sudden fear came to the woman on the hillside.

'Come back!' she called. 'You will be burnt yourself.'

For a moment Hans hesitated. Did he hear her? Or was he but searching for a firm foothold?

Gingerly, he placed one foot on an ashen pile. It seemed safe enough. He leaned his weight upon it and peered for the brute's remains.

His wife's warning scream came too late.

A pile of blackened bricks fell with a crash beside him, and the ground seemed to open under his feet. With a startled cry the old man flung up his arms and plunged forward – forward and *downward!*

A shower of red-hot debris sparked all about him. A rush of cold air raced past his ears. With a mighty splash Hans struck the icy water of the mill's underground cistern. He was trapped.

Coughing and spluttering, he came up to the surface and began to swim. If only he could keep up until his wife came or brought help.

An iron bar projected from the side of the well. He made for it with the heavy, deliberate strokes of an ageing man. If he could cling to that . . .

A sudden swirl in the water brought his head round with a jerk It was dark down here. Only the glow of the smoking timbers up above illuminated the dank moss-strewn walls.

He screwed up his eyes with the effort to see.

Splash!

There it was again! Nearer this time. Something slithering in the darkness. Over to his left. He drew himself up by his bar and peered.

Something was heaving up out of the water beside him. It seemed as though it would never stop. Higher and higher it grew until it loomed gigantic over him. IT turned its head.

With a shriek he loosened the bar and struck out. The Monster was alive – *alive!*

Like a streak a giant paw clamped on the withered neck, thrusting it down – down. There was a feeble struggle, a gurgle, the splash of beating limbs against water – and Hans lay still. Then with a wordless roar of animal fury, Frankenstein's Monster lifted the drowned body in its arms and hurled it blindly at the wall.

The skull cracked and the corpse slipped out of sight; and at the same moment from the ruins above there sounded the voice of the dead man's wife.

'Are you there, Hans? Hans, where are you? Hans!'

The Monster's lips parted in a crack of fiendish glee and an unholy light gleamed from behind its loathsome eyes. The red glow from the embers illumined its face as it groped – upward, upward –

Raising itself still higher it reached a paw through a crack in the ruins. The woman grasped it.

'Oh, thank God, Hans!' she gasped. 'There you are. Wait, and I'll pull you up.'

Back in the Schloss von Frankenstein there was rejoicing. Young Baron Frankenstein had regained consciousness for the first time since the Monster's murderous assault.

He looked up with gratitude in his eyes as he saw his wife bending over him, and guessed that it was thanks to her nursing that he was better.

Elizabeth Frankenstein and Minnie, her maid, guarded him jealously, and soon he was well on the way to recovery.

Naturally enough, feeling his strength return, he hankered to go on with his experiments. But on one point Elizabeth was firm. There was to be no more ghoulish tampering with the dead.

'Forget all that horror,' she implored him. 'It was never meant that we should know those things – the secrets of life and death.'

Her husband looked at her fondly. Heaven knew that he loved her – that he would do most things in his power to please her. But to abandon research just now, when he had achieved the superhuman? Ah, no, he argued, it was unfair of her to ask.

'I dreamed of being the first to give to the world the secret of which God is so jealous,' he told her, sitting in the great panelled room which was his favourite. 'I yearned for the formula for Life.' A light came into his eyes, and he went on eagerly: 'Think of the power it gave me – to create a man! And I did it! Who knows, in time I might have trained him to do my will. I could have bred a race!'

Gently Elizabeth smoothed his brow, smiling when she saw the wrinkles melt. But there was an undercurrent of fear in her voice as she warned him.

'Henry, don't say those things. Don't think them – as you love me.'

She knew that Frankenstein had ever longed for power. Now that he had achieved the warped ambition on which he had set his heart, she dreaded the overwhelming brilliance of his brain.

Many times they talked together like this, and frequently she urged Frankenstein to yield to her wish to go abroad far from the scene of his vile creation.

But late one night, when the wind howled like a thousand tortured devils round the tall battlements of the castle, there came a knock at the heavy oak door which shattered forever the hope that was dawning in Elizabeth's heart.

It was Minnie who answered the summons. A queer, tall man smiled down at her. There was that in his glittering eyes which struck terror as she backed involuntarily before him. Somehow she knew instinctively that he had come for no good purpose.

'Tell the Baron Frankenstein that Doctor Pretorius is here on a secret matter of grave importance,' said the stranger, not unmusically. 'Tell him that I must see him alone – to-night.'

Minnie's scared glance flickered up and down the long black cloak which wrapped the stranger. It reminded her of the pall which had covered her father's coffin. She shivered.

'The master's a-bed,' she quavered, flinching despite herself under the tall man's gaze. 'That's where all decent folk should be at this time of night.'

'So?' Pretorius' long teeth gleamed wolfishly in the moonlight as he grinned at her discomfiture. 'Nevertheless he will see me.' And with a thrust of his hand he was past Minnie and in the hall.

Pretorius was right. Frankenstein knew him well. He was a Doctor of Philosophy who had been dismissed his University for dabbling in Black Art.

He saw him at once. In the world of science in which he moved there were many less creditable persons with whom he had had to do business.

Pretorius came straight to the point. He knew all about Frankenstein's monster and complimented him upon its creation. But, he added, he had also succeeded in producing Life – though by a vastly different method. If the Baron would accompany him he would be delighted to show him the results of his experiments.

'What is behind all this?' asked Frankenstein at last. It was plain that the doctor was wrestling with some secret excitement.

Pretorius' lips parted in their wolfish grin.

'Don't you see?' he said. 'We must work *together*. Together we may reach a goal undreamed of.'

Again he urged him to accompany him back to his laboratory.

Feebly Frankenstein clung to his promise to Elizabeth.

'No, I'm through with it all. I'm going away,' he said.

His tone transformed the other.

Savagely Pretorius clutched him by the arm. The mask came off and he showed himself in his true colours as a threatening blackmailer.

'Do you know that your monster is still at large?' he challenged. 'That it has already done two more murders since its resurrection?'

Frankenstein stared aghast, and the doctor went on:

'Luckily, few apart from your wife and myself know that you are responsible for its existence. But there are penalties, I would remind you, for killing people. If I were to tell the law who made this roving instrument of death –'

Frankenstein paled and frowned.

'Are you threatening me?' he asked haughtily.

Again came that wolfish grin.

'Ah, no! Don't put it so crudely. Say rather that I am reminding you it were better that we work – *together*!'

For a moment there was silence, then Frankenstein rose to his feet and rang the bell. To the man who came he gave orders for his carriage to be made ready. Then he turned to Pretorius.

'Damn you!' he muttered. 'I have no choice. Let us go.'

He soon found that the doctor had not exaggerated. He had produced Life as he had claimed, and in his laboratory were some half-dozen pigmy men and women – all living and imprisoned in flasks.

'While you were digging in your graves,' Pretorius explained, 'and piecing together dead tissues – I went to the source of Life. I grew my creatures.'

'They are perfect!' exclaimed Frankenstein, scientifically enthusiastic in spite of himself. 'But what a pity they are so small.'

Pretorius nodded encouragingly.

'Ah, there I give you best. You *did* achieve size. But don't you agree, my friend, that we should make an astonishing collaboration?'

For some tense moments love of science and love for his wife warred within Frankenstein's breast. Pretorius guessed that the battle needed but one more thrust to turn the way he wanted.

'Think,' he whispered eagerly. 'Our dream is but half realised.

Alone you have created a man – now, together we shall make him a mate.'

'You mean – ?'

Pretorius nodded slowly.

'Yes – a woman.'

The light of fanaticism gleamed in Frankenstein's eyes.

Even as they were discussing this unholy partnership the Monster was stumbling over fields and pasture land. It was thirsty and famished.

Hitherto, Life had shown it only brutality, so that it lived by the code of Fear. If it could frighten, it had soon learned that it could take what it wanted. If in its turn it could be made to fear – it fled.

Somehow the blood pumping through the long-dead tissues of its body was bringing back feeling to its nerves. Dully, like a clogged engine, its brain was learning to work – to think. Dimly it realised that it was an outcast – a horror to other men, for the meaning of stray remarks was permeating its befogged mind.

The sun rose over the hills, lighting the tree-tops with a golden sheen. The monster, weary, paused in its path. It needed drink. The sound of sheep bleating floated towards it, and it ambled slowly in the direction of the sound. There was blood in the bodies of sheep.

Suddenly, rounding a bend, it saw her – a woman-thing. She was standing on a rock by the side of a stream and about her her sheep were scattered. A stream! – Water! The creature quickened its pace.

The shepherdess did not see the Monster until it was almost upon her. Her first intimation of its presence was the strange snarl which served it for speech. She turned – then aghast at the horrid spectacle mowing and posturing before her, she screamed in abject terror and fainted dead away.

How could she tell that the queer noises it made were a pathetic attempt to reassure her?

Angrily the Monster bent over her. This faint was something it had not seen before. It did not understand it. It struck irritably at the inanimate girl . . .

Crack!

From the distance came the sound of a shot. The Monster uttered a growl of pain and clasped its arm. Then, drawing back its taut skin above its yellow fangs, it roared its fury.

The two huntsmen who had seen it strike the girl conferred hastily. Again a gun was raised. Instinct or intelligence was awakening in the Monster. It ducked and fled incontinent into a nearby wood.

*

'Well, well, what is it?'

The burgomaster looked up irritably from his desk as a man, panting and dishevelled, burst unceremoniously into his room. Behind him, mouthing startled protests, stood the burgomaster's servant.

The intruder gulped for breath. He swayed, exhausted with his long run.

'The Monster!' he gasped, clutching blindly at a chair for support. 'He's in the woods. A friend and I were out shooting – we saw him attacking a girl. My friend fired. I think he hit him.'

'The Monster, you say? Excellent!' It was the moment for which the pompous old burgomaster had been waiting. For years he had been longing to show the good people of Ingolstadt the kind of stuff of which he was made. He turned to his servant.

'Stop gibbering, man! Get out the bloodhounds. Raise all the men you can. Lock the women indoors and wait for me.' Fuming, he reached for his gun on the wall.

Outside the house he could hear his servant shouting the news. In a minute the narrow street was packed with a jostling throng of excited villagers, all armed haphazard with guns, pitchforks, crowbars and anything else to which they could lay their hands.

Headed by the burgomaster, they trooped out of the village.

They came to the spot where the other huntsman stood supporting the frightened shepherdess in his arms.

'Which way did he go?'

Even before he could answer the burgomaster's question the bloodhounds were baying and straining at the leash.

'That way. Hurry!'

Howling threats, the rabble plunged into a neighbouring thicket.

The hounds nosed the ground, their breath coming in quick, eager sniffs. They moved silently, swiftly, leading the mob off the rough cart track and up a steep, pine-covered slope.

Suddenly from the ranks of the crowd there came a cry.

'There he is!'

'Faster, faster!'

The burgomaster shaded his eyes. Ahead, just breasting the top of the hill, a vast, misshapen figure was loping. It ran awkwardly, as though its man-made limbs were unequal to the task. They moved ponderously like primitive metal pistons.

In a trice the hounds had reached it, and stood round baying while the rest of the human pack came up.

Snarling, the great creature faced them, its pallid lips drawn back above huge yellow fangs. It lunged out savagely, grunting and squealing like a tormented pig. Fœtid green froth dripped from its gaping mouth.

But there were too many this time for Frankenstein's creation to tackle. Someone slipped behind it. A thwack from an iron bar struck it on the head. It screamed with the pain. A well-aimed stone brought it to its knees.

One, more daring than the rest, stepping forward from the throng, slipped a rope about its neck. Striking, stabbing, kicking, the crowd closed in. The memory of murdered wives and children banished all pity.

'Bind him securely!' bellowed the burgomaster from a safe distance. 'Tie his feet first – then lash him to a pole. There are plenty of fallen pines about here.'

Groaning and writhing, the Monster was subdued, lashed to a fallen tree and carried down the hill. There he was thrust into a farm wagon and brought back in triumph to Ingolstadt.

In the dungeon of the prison a small gang of men had stayed to make the place proof against the Monster's gargantuan strength. A gigantic chair had been prepared with rings of iron, into which its feet and hands were now thrust. An immense iron collar was welded about its neck, and a steel chain twisted about its body secured it to staples driven into the wall.

At last the burgomaster stepped back satisfied.

'That will hold him. What a pity I can't act further without orders from my superiors!' He looked round for his secretary. 'Heinrich! – Where the devil's he got to?' The man came forward. 'Ah, I want you to take a letter to Geneva.'

With a smirk of triumph the burgomaster went out. Behind him he heard the shock of the heavy bolts of the dungeon thudding into place.

Each side of the metal-studded door two guards stationed themselves. Both were armed.

The burgomaster smirked again. Yes, it was a clever capture. It should mean the mayoral chain for him – that is, if these fool villagers had any gratitude!

Scarcely had he begun to dictate his letter, however, when a terrific uproar in the street outside called him to the window. He called down angrily:

'Ungrateful wretches! What is it now?'

A fusillade of shots scattered the crowd before they could answer him, and a screaming woman fell wounded in the roadway. The burgomaster thrust his head farther out and withdrew it hurriedly.

Down the centre of the road, roaring with shrill animal fury, came the Monster. About its neck, wrists and ankles were rough abrasions where the shackles had clasped its flesh. Its eyes glared wildly and its teeth gnashed as it raced after the scared villagers who had so lately been its captors.

Stooping, it swooped upon the prostrate woman, snapping her spine in its two hands as easily as a man might break a twig. It shook the body venomously before flinging it brutally down on to the cobbles. The skull split open and the Monster trampled viciously upon the dead white face until its leaden boots were spattered with vivid gouts of blood.

'Shoot!' screamed the burgomaster helplessly from his window. The red-tape which had prevented him from having the creature killed on sight vanished. With it fled his hopes of the mayoralty. His natural pomposity was forgotten in the sudden wave of horror which overcame him. Cursing, he ran to the wall where he had just replaced his gun.

When he returned it was in time to see the Monster lumbering over the fields beyond the village, and in a corner of the street a little group huddled over the still body of a child.

Terror was loose again!

One by one from outlying hamlets reports came in. There was Frau Neumann wantonly and horribly murdered. A gipsy family completely wiped out. The burgomaster railed at his guards and called on Heaven, but to no purpose. No bonds could have held a creature possessing such colossal strength; and now few could be found with the courage to go after it again. Perhaps, they argued, somewhat belatedly, if they left it alone it would leave them in peace.

It was after its third murder that the Monster, wounded by a random shot and exhausted by the chase, came to a tiny hut set in the heart of a coppice.

Night was falling, and the earthy smell of the dewdrenched bracken beckoned the creature to rest awhile.

Furtively, for it had learned to fear all men, the Monster moved towards the lighted window of the hut. Then it paused, startled.

From within the little dwelling came a strange, sweet sound. Another. And another. Someone was playing a violin.

Music was a new sensation to the Monster. It was pleasant. It drew near, fascinated.

Within the hut a hermit, who was blind and old, played on unaware of the hideous face pressed close to the pane. For fully a minute the

Monster watched. Then it saw the old man turn – turn and stare mildly at him through sightless eyes that saw not the watcher's aspect and were, consequently, unafraid.

The Monster moaned faintly. It was nearly spent.

The playing ceased. As often happens when one sense is lost, another develops acutely. So it was with the blind man. The sound the Monster made struck loudly on his ears. He went to the door.

'Who is there?' he called, gently.

TWO

For a space Monster and man faced each other. The moment was tense with foreboding. What would the Monster do?

Slayer of innocents, would it strike down the helpless blind figure before it, or would it mistake the violin in his hand for an instrument of destruction and stagger away into the darkness?

The hermit came closer. He could sense where the other was standing. Gently he spoke.

'You are welcome, my friend, whoever you are. Forgive me, but I cannot see you. I am blind.'

Slowly he stretched out a hand and touched the Monster. A tense growl caused him to start back in alarm, then a sticky sensation at the tips of his fingers made him utter a low cry of concern. *Blood!* – the stranger was wounded!

Blind and unafraid, he slipped an arm about the creature and guided it into the hut. And there he tended the Monster's hurts.

That night the hermit prayed. He had long wanted a companion in his loneliness.

'Dear Father, I thank Thee,' he murmured, 'that out of the silence of the night Thou has brought two of Thy lonely children together and sent me a friend to be a light to mine eyes and a comfort in time of trouble. Amen.'

From then onward, a queer friendship sprang up between them. The hermit believed the Monster to be dumb, and the affliction gave them a mutual bond. Blindness and dumbness – each could supply a want to the other.

And the Monster? No longer hounded, stoned and treated as an outcast, it responded to the hermit's kindness with the gratitude and devotion of an injured animal.

It learned to speak.

Painfully, it struggled with the sounds the hermit taught it.

'Bread – drink – good!' These words were pleasant, happy words. They were words which brought comfort and helped to supply bodily needs. But the greatest word of all, the word which sowed the seed of a soul in the Monster's vast carcase was – *'friend.'*

'Friend,' it repeated over and over again, touching the hermit's sleeve with grateful humility. 'Friend – good!'

And here it might have stayed harmlessly for ever but for a certain happening.

There had been peace in the countryside for some months now and people were beginning to venture abroad again. The Monster was supposed to be dead. Some even claimed to have seen its giant body lying at the foot of a precipice. A great cloud seemed to have been rolled back from above the village of Ingolstadt.

One night, two strangers called at the hut. They had been out after wild duck and lost their way in the wood. With his usual courtesy, the hermit asked them in to rest and eat. They entered.

Suddenly one of them uttered a low cry and pointed to a huge shape that sat hunched in a corner.

'Look!' he gasped. 'It's the Monster!'

With an oath the other leaped to his feet and raised his gun. But he was not quick enough.

Association with the hermit had sharpened the Monster's intelligence. Though as yet it could talk but little, it understood all that was said. And it knew that the word 'Monster' was never applied to it by a 'friend.'

With a hideous cry it sprang, wresting the gun from the startled man and hurling him back against the wall. The next instant it had sent the weapon flying through the window.

Bewildered, the poor hermit raised his voice.

'What are you doing?' he cried anxiously. 'This is my friend.'

The men turned on him furiously.

'Friend? Why this is the fiend which has been murdering half the countryside. Good Heavens, can't you see?'

Then, looking closer, they realised what had happened. The hermit was blind. He did not know.

But there was no time now for explanations. The Monster, roused from its feeling of security, meant to remove the two strangers who had blundered out the truth in the only way it understood. Lifting the table as easily as a matchbox, it flung it savagely across the hut.

It caught the second man as he was shifting his gun from his shoulder, knocking him back against the door. The impact brought the swinging lamp down from its staple in the roof and a wave of flame shot up. In three seconds the hut was ablaze.

Both men tugged at the hermit, dragging him out of harm's way. Then they, too, leaped for the open door. Within the hut the Monster battled frenziedly with the flames, hurling himself again and again at the wall in the attempt to break it down – anything to get out of the furnace which was raging all about it.

At last with a crash a board gave. Another and another. Screaming with pain and fury, the creature plunged through the opening and out into the wood. The hunt was on again.

A black shape stood silent by the gaping mouth of a tomb. It was tall and gaunt, and the pallid moonlight shining from above, gleamed on a row of yellow teeth set in a wolfish grin.

All about it, like stark fingers pointing to the sky, rose countless headstones, while here and there a monument to some noble family towered grimly remindful above its neighbours. It amused Doctor Pretorius to think that even in death there was snobbery.

The graveyard was deserted, as a graveyard should be at dead of night, save for this solitary figure who waited motionless beside the crypt.

Somewhere an owl hooted. The Doctor turned his head, then his lips snapped with an exclamation of annoyance as he noted the glimmer of a light moving over the graves. Of what use all this secrecy when the fools gave their presence away in this idiotic manner?

Cupping his hands, he uttered an answering hoot and waited until the two men came up.

'Put out that light,' he hissed, as they stood together awkwardly before him. 'We want no witnesses for what we have to do.'

Reluctantly, for the men he had hired were superstitious peasants, they obeyed him. One of them blew out the lantern and the three figures stood listening intently.

No sound, however, fell upon their ears, save the moan of the night breeze in the tall trees fringing the cemetery and the occasional creak of their branches.

Satisfied at last that they were unobserved, Doctor Pretorious led the way down the narrow stone steps to the bowels of the crypt.

To-night was an important one for Pretorius. He had threatened, wrangled, cajoled and pleaded with Frankenstein for his co-operation in the experiment which was to make a woman fit to mate with the Monster. But it had all been to no purpose. Just when he had believed that Frankenstein was ready to yield, that his enthusiasm and love of science would compel him to throw in his lot with him, Elizabeth had entered the room.

The few words that she had heard as she entered the door had been sufficient to enlighten her as to what was proceeding, and she had immediately forbidden her husband to countenance the thought of another such experiment. What was more – she had shown the Doctor the door and given orders for the Schloss to be closed while she and Frankenstein undertook a long trip abroad together.

It was necessary, therefore, that Pretorius should conduct his experiment alone, and it was to procure a suitable body for the attempt that he was here in this crypt to-night.

At the foot of the steps he paused and re-lit the lantern. The pale light flickered fitfully, dimmed and glowed. Like a great crow, draped in his long black cloak, Pretorius lifted the lantern on high and sniffed. The rank earthy smell of the grave assailed his nostrils. He grinned appreciatively. He was in his element.

He looked about him. Behind him his assistants shivered apprehensively.

The coffins were arranged in tiers. Some of them were incredibly old. Mildewed and rotting, they had warped with the damp, and where they had warped they gaped, disclosing yellow bones or torn and fibrous shrouds.

Into one of these Pretorius thrust his hand. When he withdrew it, it clasped a woman's skull. He chuckled softly, patting the bony cheek with insolent familiarity. Then he tossed it playfully at the shrinking men, deriding their horror as it smashed to pieces like an egg on the cold stone floor.

'She's no use to me,' he muttered, tearing down a huge festoon of cobwebs which hung from the ceiling with his bare hands. 'Too old. Too small.'

A fat spider scuttled across his foot. He stamped upon it. It squelched, and he wrinkled his nose with distaste as he thrust its remains aside with his boot.

'I want someone young,' he continued, peering at the inscriptions on the coffin lids. 'A girl – beautiful, supple, recently dead – and unmarked from any injury.'

The two men stirred uneasily.

Taking a wall each, they began to inspect the coffins. Presently one of them called out, his voice booming strangely beneath the vaulted ceiling.

'Will *she* do?'

Pretorius hurried to his side.

'Read the inscription. How old was she?'

Stooping, the man began to read.

'Madeline Ernestine, beloved daughter of –'

'Skip that.' Pretorius' voice was sharp. 'How *old* was she?'

'Aged nineteen years and three months.'

'Good! That's the one. Break open the coffin.'

The two men hesitated and glanced at each other. A sudden glint came into the Doctor's eyes. It was a glint akin to madness. His fingers worked.

'Well, what are you waiting for?' he asked in a dangerously soft tone.

The two men shivered and crossed themselves. Their fear was abject. Pretorius grinned wickedly.

'Do you want me to send you to the gallows – where you belong?' he reminded gently. 'Do not forget that I know who murdered Julius Steinberg.'

The hold he had over them had its effect. Muttering, they bent over the girl's coffin, hacking and prising, until a few moments later with a rending sound the lid came away.

Gloating, Pretorius leaned over the still form within.

'Pretty little thing,' he chuckled, cutting the winding sheets from about her face. 'I hope her bones are firm.'

Caressingly he ran his fingers over the dead limbs.

The two men picked up their tools, and, at a sign from the Doctor, made their way out of this abode of death. The lantern they left burning on the bottom step. It was enough for them to breathe once more the pure fresh air of the world above, and with all haste they flitted gratefully across the graveyard, leaving their erstwhile employer with the corpse.

Alone, Pretorius seated himself upon the coffin, while he raised the slender body in his arms. She was not heavy, despite her dead weight. He propped her up against a wall while he lit a cigar and awaited the arrival of his own servant. Between them they would convey the corpse to his laboratory. There was half an hour at least to wait.

The lantern burned lower.

Pretorius was alone now, save for the silent occupants of the shelves about him. His isolation did not trouble him in the least. Cynical, indifferent to life and death, he was enthusiastic only in the matter of research. This subject, however, whipped his imagination to the point of madness, and he was entirely at a loss to understand how it was that Frankenstein, who had succeeded so far, could fail to pursue his crazy dream to the limit.

If only he could think of a way to force his hand!

Musing, Pretorius puffed out dense volumes of cigar smoke. They assumed strange shapes in the failing light.

'Alone – I am still a pioneer,' he muttered to the corpse that faced him. 'I may fail at any turn. But with Frankenstein, whose creature still walks somewhere on this earth, to help me, ah, my pretty morsel, what a nuptial I could arrange for you!'

As though it heard and understood, the head of the corpse dropped forward. The Doctor's eyes narrowed, then he laughed softly as he noted the cause.

A giant rat falling with a soft plop from the ceiling had struck the body on the shoulder in its passage, slightly dislodging it. Glancing malevolently at the Doctor with beady eyes, it scuttled across the flagged floor and disappeared.

Chuckling to himself, Doctor Pretorius sat back and blew another smoke-ring. Then he delved into his pocket for his watch. What a devil of a time the fellow was in coming, to be sure!

A creak sounded at the far end of the crypt. Surely that was he?

Pretorius prepared to rise, when suddenly it dawned upon him that the noise emanated from that part of the crypt farthest from the entrance. It could not, therefore, be his servant. It must be *someone else!*

For a moment his heart leaped, and a thousand superstitious fears inherited through the ages came to plague him. The next instant reason conquered, and he was his emotionless self again.

The sound was repeated. It was louder this time.

To the Doctor's straining ears it sounded like a heavy weight being cautiously lowered to the floor. It dragged slightly.

Slowly he turned his head. Then, with an exclamation of complete surprise, he sprang to his feet.

There, close behind him, its body almost completely out of a coffin, was the Monster. It had obviously lain hidden there all the time the two men had been working in the crypt. Slowly it swayed to its feet and lurched towards the Doctor.

It was to Pretorius' credit that, after the first shock of surprise was over, he was unafraid. He regarded the creature coolly but warily. Indeed, a certain studied insolence crept into his voice as he addressed it.

'Oh, I thought I was alone,' he said airily. 'Good evening.'

The flickering light from the dying lantern picked out the bones on the creature's face. They gleamed yellow-white under the taut skin. Pretorius watched it guardedly as it drew a step nearer. For weeks it had been missing – who knew what subtle changes might have taken place in the man-made creature. Its next action sent the hair rising up on the Doctor's prosaic head. It spoke.

'Friend?' asked the Monster. Its voice was harsh and sepulchral.

Pretorius took a grip on himself. After all, it was all perfectly normal. The Monster had been in the world some while now. It was natural that it should have learned to imitate human speech.

'Indeed, I hope so,' responded the Doctor, his brain beginning to work rapidly. He indicated a seat beside him. 'Have some refreshment?'

Avidly the Monster swallowed the wine and food that Pretorius had brought for himself. It was a wise move on the Doctor's part. It put the creature in a good humour.

Peering about it with curiousity, its gaze lighted on the corpse of the girl. It turned to Pretorius.

'You make man, like me?' it asked. There was a pathetic eagerness in its harsh notes.

Pretorius shook his head.

'No,' he replied, playing up. 'Woman – friend for you.'

The Monster nodded, gratified.

'Woman? Friend? I want friend, like me,' it said.

The idea which had been simmering in the Doctor's brain from the moment he set eyes on the Monster and learned that it could speak, suddenly fructified. Stroking his chin, he rose to his feet.

'I think you can be very useful, my friend,' he smiled. 'You can add a little force to my argument, if necessary.'

For a moment he hesitated, then: 'Do you know who Henry Frankenstein is?' he asked. 'And who you are?'

The Monster nodded.

'Made me – from dead. I love dead – hate living.'

Pretorius chuckled.

'You are wise in your generation,' he answered. 'Well, we must have a long talk, you and I. And then I have an important call to make. Perhaps Baron Frankenstein will not, after all, be so selfish as to refuse my request – when he sees you face to face.'

There and then in the blackness of the tomb – for the light had gone out long before they finished – Pretorius told the Monster about his plan to make a mate, emphasising Frankenstein's refusal and appealing for the creature's co-operation. And when at last he stumbled up the steps into the graveyard above, it was with the knowledge that the Monster understood its part in his plan and could be relied upon to do its share well.

Immediately Pretorius made his way to the Schloss von Frankenstein. Despite the lateness of the hour, Minnie was awake.

'I must see the Baron,' declared the Doctor, pacing the hall. 'Immediately.'

Protesting that her master and mistress were unable to see anybody, Minnie left him. But the clangour of the great door bell had alarmed Frankenstein.

'What is it?' he called from the library.

'It's that Doctor Pretorius again. He wants to see you,' Minnie answered.

Frankenstein groaned and turned to his wife.

'Then I knew it. Shall I never have any peace from the man?' He went to the door and addressed Minnie. 'Send him away. I won't see him.'

Minnie turned, then she gasped. Silently the Doctor had come up behind her.

'Good evening, Baron,' he said pleasantly.

For the moment Frankenstein was too aghast at the man's effrontery to say anything. His wife took command.

'Dr Pretorius,' she said icily. 'I don't know what your business at this time of night may be – but whatever it is it will have to wait. My husband and I are leaving almost immediately.'

Pretorius refused to be ruffled. He bowed with mock courtesy and turned to Frankenstein.

'I think you know why I have come, Henry,' he said with meaning. 'If the Baroness will leave us a moment –'

Elizabeth and Frankenstein exchanged glances. He nodded and she gathered her wrap about her.

'I will await you in my room,' she told him, then beckoned to the waiting maid. 'Come, Minnie.'

Alone, the two men faced each other. 'I have completed by my method a perfect human brain,' announced the Doctor. 'It is living, but dormant. Everything is ready – for *us*.'

Frankenstein shook his head.

'No!' he said. 'I won't do it – that's my final word!'

Pretorius smiled. Again there was a hint of the wolf in his expression. Slowly he crossed the library to the french window and beckoned.

'I expected this,' he said. 'So I have brought my other assistant, who may persuade you to change your mind.'

As if hypnotised, Frankenstein stared at the french window, which was gradually opening. Then, with a cry of fear, he fell back, hands out-stretched.

The Monster, hideous creature of his own making, stood before him. With one massive paw it pointed to a chair. Its harsh voice filled the room.

'Frankenstein – sit down!' it said.

Pretorius began to chuckle.

'Yes, there have been developments, you see. He can talk.'

Something in the creature's malevolent leer as it gazed at him chilled the man who had made it. He called out piteously.

'What do you want?'

The Monster came closer.

'You know,' it said.

Pretorius intervened.

'He wants a woman – a friend – a mate. You'll help us make one now, won't you, Frankenstein?'

Dumbly the scientist shook his head. The Monster growled. It advanced threateningly.

'Yes – *must!*' it ordered.

Frankenstein cowered under the upraised fist. To think that he had made this Thing – which was now commanding him as if *It* were master!

He appealed to Pretorius.

'Get him out!' he cried. 'I won't even discuss it till he's gone.'

Ponderously the Monster turned its head until it looked squarely at the Doctor. Back in the recesses if its brain it knew that there was something it had to do – something pre-arranged between them. Pretorius gave the sign. Stiffly the creature turned and marched back the way it had come. The french window swung wide as it passed through into the moonlight, its tattered rags flapping in the breeze – and with it went the stench of the tomb.

Ashen pale, Frankenstein wiped the sweat from his brow.

'Now,' said Pretorius with a grin, 'let me explain my method and benefit from your experience.'

Frankenstein sat as though carved in stone, while the Doctor talked. Elizabeth meant more to him than anything in the world, and she had extracted his promise. If he agreed to this devilish proposal, he knew that he might be loosing yet another murderer upon the world – who knew, if not in time – a race of murderers? Yet if he refused?

Pretorius was speaking.

'I have, my friend,' he was saying, 'an excellent laboratory installed within a ruined tower high on a hill. It is not far from here. There we can conduct our mutual experiment in seclusion. I can assure you there will be no dearth of fresh bodies, for I have in my employ –'

He broke off, and his mouth slowly widened into that terribly wolfish grin. From somewhere above them a terrible scream had rung out. It reverberated down the castle corridor.

It came again. And again.

Frankenstein leaped to his feet, his face suddenly grey.

'My God!' he muttered. 'That's Elizabeth's voice.'

The next instant he was racing up the great stone stairs.

At the head of the stairs he met Minnie. She was shaking with terror. Fear glared from her eyes and for a moment she could not speak. He seized her roughly.

'What's happened! Quickly! Tell me!'

The grip of his fingers brought back her courage, and she moistened her frozen lips. Then:

'My lady!' she moaned. 'Oh, my lady – the Monster's got her!' With a trembling finger she pointed out of the window. They crowded round it.

Scaling the wall of the courtyard as easily as if it were a ditch was the Monster. Even as they watched, it began to lope down the hill. The light of the moon threw its grotesque shadow after it like some great black demon dancing with fiendish glee. And from Frankenstein's throat there rasped a despairing cry as the moon showed something else across the Monster's shoulder – the body of a woman, slender and white and limp – the body of Elizabeth, his wife!

'Now, perhaps, you will do what he asks,' whispered Pretorius in his ear. 'It is the only way to save her.'

THREE

It was true – and Frankenstein knew it. The only way to save Elizabeth was to throw in his lot with Pretorius and accede to the Monster's demands.

The Monster wanted a mate. Very well, it should have one.

There was but one thing for which Frankenstein stipulated before he set to work, and that was to hear his wife's voice that he might know she was safe and unharmed. To this Pretorius agreed.

Together they went to the ruined tower on the hill where the doctor had his laboratory. There Frankenstein was allowed to speak to his wife by means of a kind of telephone.

'Elizabeth,' he cried eagerly into the mouthpiece. 'Are you safe?'

He could scarcely speak for the relief when he recognised her beloved voice answering him.

'Henry! – Yes, darling I'm quite safe – but oh! the dark and this dreadful –'

There was a noise at the other end of the wire. Frankenstein held his breath, straining his ears to listen. Her voice came again.

'I'm quite near – in a cave. Come for me –'

It broke off with a gasp. Then, shrilling in his ear he heard the words: 'Oh, God, it's here! It's here! – Henry!' Silence followed.

Distracted, Frankenstein shouted down the instrument. There was no reply. Impotent to do anything, he looked up and found Doctor Pretorius smiling sardonically at him.

'My dear friend,' murmured the doctor, 'you surely did not believe Elizabeth's gaoler would be so foolish as to permit her to betray her whereabouts? But rest assured, so long as you do what is asked of you she will come to no harm.'

Frankenstein knew when he was beaten. Subdued at last, he bent himself to his task.

It was not long before the scientist in him rose uppermost and he was working day and night at a bench littered with strange apparatus. Test-tubes, retorts, queer metallic globes and intricate dials, all had their part in fashioning what was to be the heart of this man-made woman.

And over him all the time, urging, encouraging threatening, stood the Monster.

A queer place was this ruined tower where Pretorius had his laboratory. It was shaped like a tall cone some hundred and fifty feet in height.

The laboratory itself occupied the ground floor, and the hollow tube of the tower leading to the starlit vault overhead formed a kind of lift-shaft. Strange and complicated machinery hung suspended from beams in the wall, or stretched trellis-like up to the castellated top of the building. The only lights were flares or arc-lamps.

*

Came the time when the current was applied and the mechanical heart began to beat. Pretorius bent his head exulting over the glass container, watching while the blood pumped steadily up and out. Suddenly, the heart fluttered and stopped.

With a curse, Frankenstein flung the contents of a bubbling crucible on to the stone floor and slumped into a chair.

'We need another heart!' he cried. 'A human heart. It must be sound and young. Where can we get it?'

The doctor and the Monster exchanged glances, then Pretorius went to the door.

'Karl!' he called.

A loutish misshapen brute appeared. Frankenstein recognised him as the doctor's most trusted servant. He began to explain.

'What we need is a female victim of sudden death. Can you do it? There are always accidental deaths occurring.'

For a moment Karl hesitated, then the doctor spoke and there was that in his eyes which made his meaning clear.

'Yes, Karl,' he nodded. 'There are always *accidental* deaths occur-ing.'

The man withdrew.

And that night a youth was mourning his sweetheart and a new heart – a human heart – beat strongly in Frankenstein's glass container.

For nine hours the small heart beat with the regularity of the normal. Excitement ran high. Taking it in turns, Pretorius and Frankenstein watched the indicator rising and falling; saw the blood began to flow simply and easily through the valves.

At last it was decided that the time had come to transfer the organ to the waiting corpse. The vital stages of the excitement had arrived.

It was an occasion when the slightest slip might mean the undoing of all their work. The Monster had served its purpose. It had kept Frankenstein from prowling in search of his wife. It was now in danger of becoming something of a nuisance. Accordingly Pretorius drugged the creature and left it lying on its great straw bed.

What was needed for the successful completion of their task was a terrible thunderstorm. Then, claimed Frankenstein, the air would be full of electricity, which could be imparted to the corpse by means of a wire attached to two kites and passing through an electrical diffuser.

Pretorius looking out of the window noted with satisfaction that such a storm was brewing this night.

'We must work quickly!' he cried, wheeling the stiff body under the bright lights of the arcs. Together they bent over it, cutting away the surgical bandages which swathed the entire figure. Soon it was ready to receive the heart.

Poising a scalpel above the breast the doctor made a swift incision and, his fingers working with all thé deft skill of which he was capable, Frankenstein inserted the beating organ.

They worked in a tense silence until the deed was finished. The atmosphere grew clammy.

'The storm is almost overhead,' announced Pretorius presently, peering out of the window. 'It will break soon.' He turned almost affectionately to the figure lying still upon the operating table. 'To think that within that skull,' he murmured, 'is an artificially developed human brain – each cell waiting for the life that is to come.'

A low rumble of thunder brought his sentence to a close. He glanced up the funnel of the high tower.

'Are the kites ready?' called Frankenstein.

'Yes.'

'Then send them up as soon as the wind rises. They must reach their zenith before they are struck.'

For some minutes longer they worked together, connecting the wires of the cosmic diffuser to the body on the table. Up on the battlements of the high tower, their shadows dancing grotesquely in the light of the paraffin flares, two men wrestled with the giant windlass which was to hold the kites when they cast off. A blue wave of lightning flickered over the mountain ridge to the south. Thicker and thicker grew the atmosphere. It felt like an immense blanket pressing down upon the world beneath.

Then came the first assault of the storm. A terrific clap of thunder which shook the valley. A vivid fork played wildly up and down the sky, and at the same time the rain began to fall.

Up the dark funnel of the hollow tower glared the white face of Frankenstein. Faintly his voice reached the men above the din of the storm.

'Stand by the kites! – Are you ready? – Let go!'

Guessing his meaning more by his gestures than by his words, they let the wires run out. The kites streamed steadily up in the wind which had mysteriously arisen to whip the raindrops fiercely into their faces. *Crash!*

With a hideous crackle the lightning stuck the kites. A beam of fire zipped down the wires holding them, down the eerie funnel of the tower to the cosmic diffuser suspended above the body. A shower of sparks played over the long-dead face and the hands of a dial began to jig rapidly.

With eyes glued to this dial Frankenstein waited while the storm raged louder and fiercer overhead. Pretorius joined him, rubbing his thin hands together nervously. He was grey with excitement, sweat dripped from his forehead, and his queer, pale eyes glinted malevolently.

Shock after shock passed through the diffuser and entered the body. The indicator on the dial rose. Forty – fifty – sixty.

Overhead the white faces of the waiting men peered down the shaft. Both had had their orders.

Suddenly Frankenstein stepped back and touched a lever.

'Ready?' he yelled. 'Stand back! It's coming up.'

There came a steady thumping from the floor below. It was the hydraulic lift at work. The table maintaining the body lurched, steadied and began to rise. Higher. And higher.

It reached the top of the tower.

Like a thousand demons let loose the storm concentrated its fury upon it. It seemed to be lit by a constant stream of lightning. Great flashes of combustible gas illuminated the shaft, jagging the darkness with flickering light.

Suddenly from one of the men on the battlements came a yell of terror.

'The Monster! It's loose! It's after me!'

Together Pretorius and Frankenstein peered upward. A gigantic shape loomed over the narrow opening far above. It picked up the screaming man, shaking him as if he had been a rat and threw him bodily over the parapet. Maddened by the sound of the storm it was running amok high up there in the battlements.

The sound of its roars reached them far below. There was no mistaking it.

'How much drug did you give him?' shouted Frankenstein in the doctor's ear.

'Enough to keep ten men under for a couple of hours more.'

Frankenstein groaned.

'Damnation! He'll ruin everything!'

But even as he spoke, a faint luminosity began to spread over the table containing the corpse above. Both noticed it together.

'Thanks Heaven! We're in time, Pretorius. Pull over that switch.'

The doctor obeyed, and with a strange hissing sound the whole devilish contraption descended.

Together they stared at the still swathed body on the table.

Forgotten now was the raging Monster overhead. They were grimed with dirt and exhausted with their efforts, but their greatest moment was yet to come. Had the experiment been a success?

Slowly, almost awfully, Frankenstein bent over the corpse. With shaking fingers he loosened the bandages covering its face. He took them off. Then he fell back gasping.

A pair of vivid blue eyes looked up at him. Strange eyes. Eyes that had in them the questing wonder of a child's and yet were filled with terror.

He turned to Pretorius.

'She lives!' he cried, triumphant. 'She lives! She *lives*!'

It was the culmination of the wildest dream. A mate had been made for the Monster.

As Pretorius and Frankenstein watched the slender figure of the girl they had created move gracefully, if a little unsteadily, across the floor of their laboratory they envisaged all that this triumph might mean.

A new race of creatures to be born in the world. Offspring of once-dead bodies. What would they be like? It was a staggering speculation.

Unlike the Monster, this girl was nearly perfect in appearance. The Monster had been the pioneer creation. It was crude and unprepossessing. All that Frankenstein had learned while making it had been utilised to this second creature's benefit. As yet, of course, she could not speak. Moaning faintly, and staring about her in terror like one barely awakened from a nightmare, she sat on a ledge by the wall of the laboratory, enduring the critical glances of her creators.

Suddenly with a queer little jerky gesture, she threw up her head and a shrill cry escaped her lips.

Following the direction of her gaze, Frankenstein gave vent to a low exclamation.

The Monster was standing in the doorway. Its face was cracked in a hideous grimace which the scientist recognised was meant to be a smile. In spite of himself, Frankenstein shuddered.

Pretorius gripped his arm.

'Sh! my friend. Watch!'

Ponderously the Monster heaved its huge bulk down the steps and into the room. Its mouth worked spasmodically. It walked straight to the staring girl.

'Friend,' it said.

The staring blue eyes grew wider. She shrank back. The two scientists watching could see fear make way for panic in the small, drawn face.

A note of anger crept into the Monster's voice.

'Friend?' it said again, reaching for the girl's hand with one gigantic paw. There was a note of command in the voice.

Something about this ghastly travesty of love sickened Frankenstein.

'Stop!' he cried.

The Monster turned with a snarl and caught the girl fiercely to him. Her mouth snapped wide and a high metallic scream rang forth. It maddened the Monster. It began to croon reassuringly to the girl, but its harsh notes only terrified her the more. She screamed again.

Swiftly Frankenstein crossed the room and took her from it. A bellow of fury escaped it.

'She hate me – like others!' mouthed the Monster. Once more it made for the girl.

At that moment there came an interruption. The door of the laboratory was flung wide and Elizabeth appeared. Finding herself unguarded, she had managed to escape.

'Henry!' she called.

Frankenstein motioned her back.

'Get out,' he cried, 'as you value your life!' He knew, none better, the temper of the Monster when roused. She shook her head.

'Not without you.'

A terrific crash told of the shattering of a trayful of glass apparatus. Smashing its way towards him, the Monster reached out once again for the girl. One paw fell for an instant on the electrical control lever.

'The lever! Look out for that lever! You'll blow us all to atoms!' shrieked Pretorius, flinging everything within reach at the raging creature.

The meaning of his words clicked in the Monster's slow intelligence. With a trumpeting roar of triumph it seized the control with both hands.

'Henry,' screamed Elizabeth again, 'you *must* come! I won't go without you.'

For a moment Frankenstein hesitated.

'I can't leave them,' he stammered. 'Don't you see –' But his hesitation gave the Monster the chance it had sought. Like a flash one huge paw shot out and seized the girl from the scientist's arms. Then it gestured savagely towards the door.

'You live!' it cried. 'Go! Go!'

Frankenstein waited no longer. And as the door slammed behind him and his wife, and the Monster saw them running madly down the hill, it caught the shrieking girl in a close embrace and threw itself flat across the lever.

'We – belong – dead!' it cried as the first shudder shook the building.

And the white, gibbering face of Dr Pretorius was the last thing it saw, before there came a blinding flash, a terrific explosion, and the whole tower thundered down in ruins.